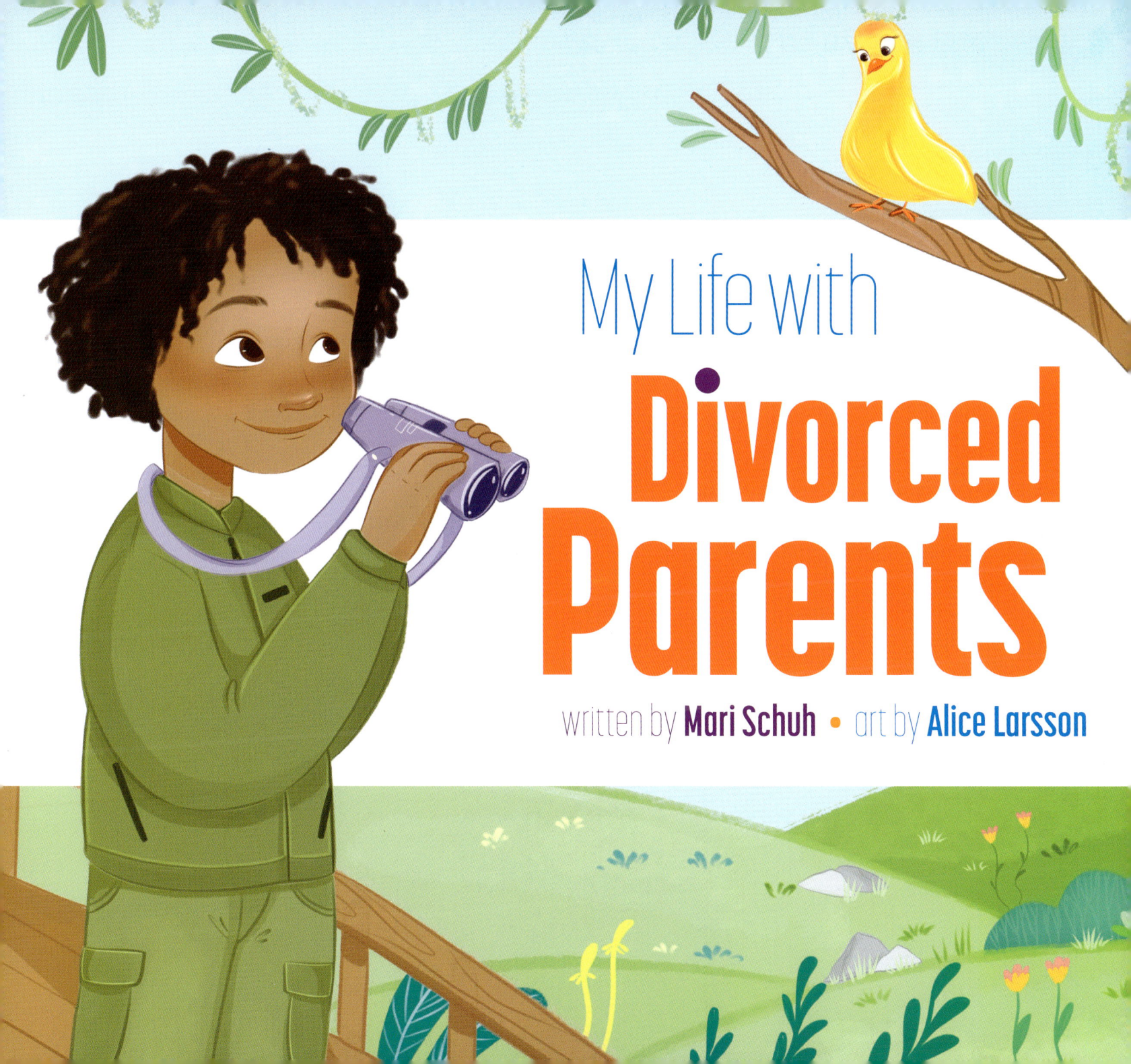

AMICUS ILLUSTRATED
is published by Amicus Learning, an imprint of Amicus
P.O. Box 227, Mankato, MN 56002
www.amicuspublishing.us

Copyright © 2025 Amicus. International copyright reserved in all countries. No part of this book may be reproduced in any form without written permission from the publisher.

Editor: Rebecca Glaser
Series Designer: Kathleen Petelinsek
Book Designer: Kim Pfeffer

Library of Congress Cataloging-in-Publication Data
Names: Schuh, Mari C., 1975- author. | Larsson, Alice, illustrator.
Title: My life with divorced parents / Mari Schuh, Alice Larsson.
Description: Mankato : Amicus Learning, 2025. | Series: My life with... | Includes bibliographical references. | Audience: Ages 6–9 | Audience: Grades 2–3 | Summary: "Meet Joseph! He likes science and animals. His parents are divorced. Joseph is real and so are his experiences. Learn about his experience with parents splitting up in this illustrated narrative nonfiction picture book for elementary students"—Provided by publisher.
Identifiers: LCCN 2023045006 (print) | LCCN 2023045007 (ebook) | ISBN 9781681529561 (paperback) | ISBN 9781645496670 (hardcover) | ISBN 9781645496939 (ebook)
Subjects: LCSH: Divorced parents—Juvenile literature. | Children of single Parents—Juvenile literature.
Classification: LCC HQ759.915 .S1535 2025 (print) | LCC HQ759.915 (ebook) | DDC 306.89—dc23/eng/20231108
LC record available at https://lccn.loc.gov/2023045006
LC ebook record available at https://lccn.loc.gov/2023045007

Printed in China

About the Author
Mari Schuh's love of reading began with cereal boxes at the kitchen table. Today she is the author of hundreds of nonfiction books for beginning readers. With each book, Mari hopes she's helping kids learn a little bit more about the world around them. Find out more about her at marischuh.com.

About the Illustrator
Alice Larsson is a London-based illustrator originally from Sweden. A natural creative, she is thrilled to be able to connect characters and stories through her work. Outside of drawing, Alice loves spending time with family and friends, as well as reading books and traveling, which sparks her creativity.

Hi! My name is Joseph. We might like some of the same things. I like to play tag. I also love science and animals. We might have some differences, too. My mom and dad are divorced. Let me tell you about my life.

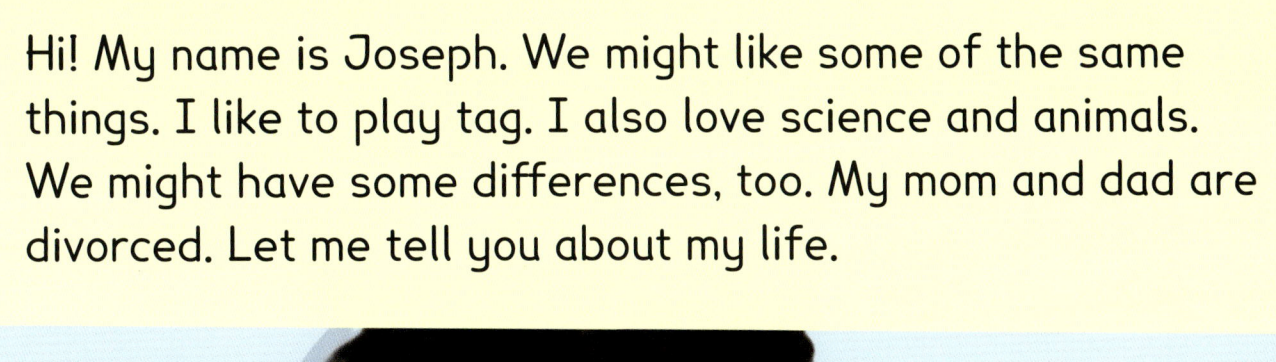

When I was very young, my family lived together. But when I was four years old, things changed. Mom and Dad did not get along well. So my four siblings, my mom, and I moved out of our home.

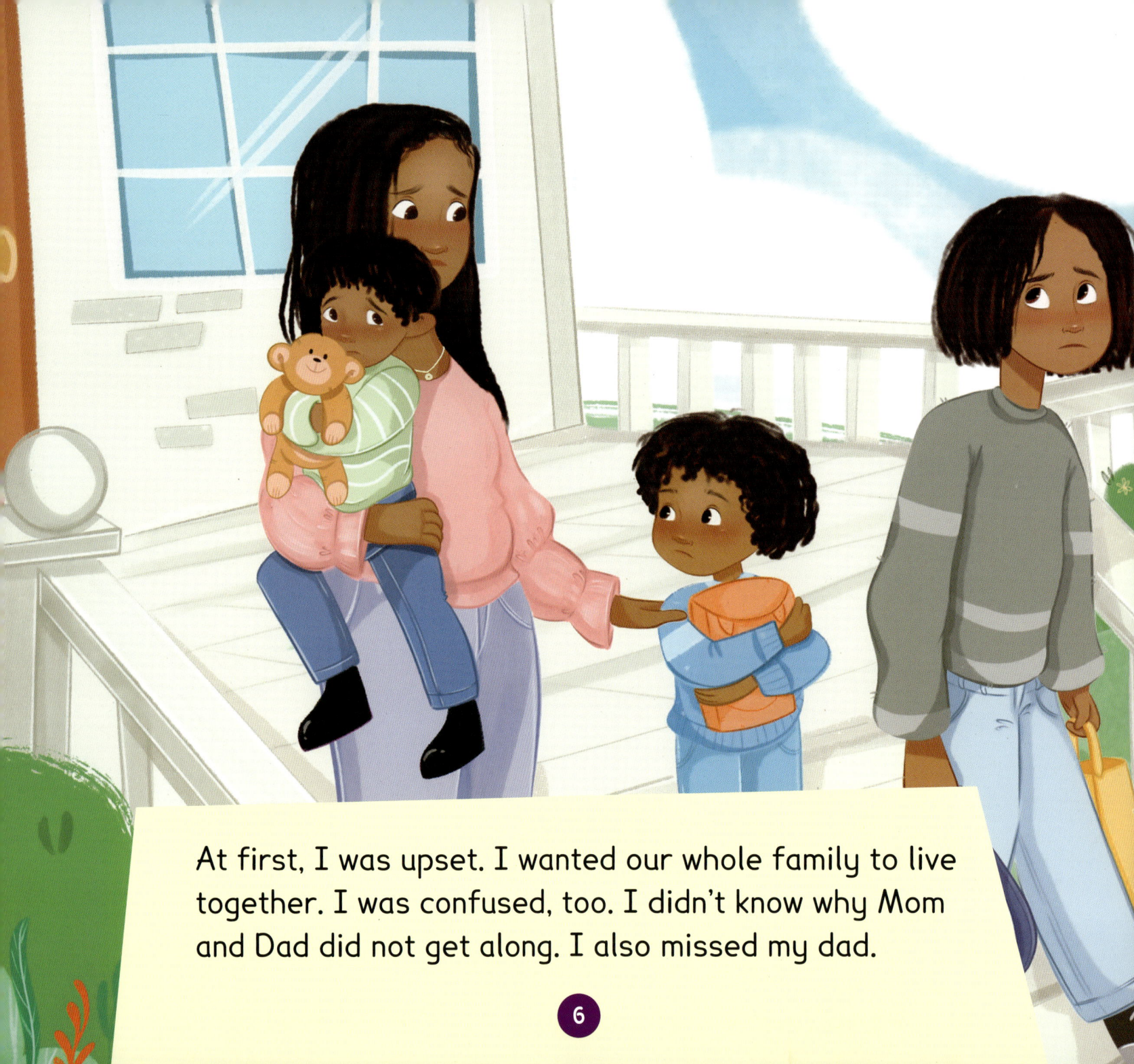

At first, I was upset. I wanted our whole family to live together. I was confused, too. I didn't know why Mom and Dad did not get along. I also missed my dad.

For three months, we stayed at a shelter. We lived apart from my dad. Mom gave me lots of hugs to help me feel better. She spent lots of time with me and my siblings.

At the shelter, I shared a room with my mom and siblings. Other people stayed at the shelter, too.

We made new friends. We ate yummy food, played games, and shared funny jokes. We listened to music, too.

Then we left the shelter and moved into a different home. My dad lived with us, too. Mom and Dad tried to get along. But it didn't work. After a few months, Dad moved out. Mom said he wasn't coming back. They were going to get a divorce.

Now, my siblings and I visit Dad every other weekend. Sometimes we see him on holidays, too. We watch TV and play video games. Dad lives with my grandma and grandpa. Grandma makes us our favorite foods. Grandpa plays soccer with us.

At home, my family is busy. We don't go to a school building. We are homeschooled. Mom is our teacher. Science is my favorite subject. I love to learn about animals. I also like math and coding.

Mom is busy, too. She runs her own business. She is very organized, which helps us all stay on track.

We help around our home. I clean the kitchen and fold laundry. Sometimes my oldest brother cooks meals for our family.

Sometimes I wish Dad was here. It would be fun to play a game with him. But I know this is how things are, and I am OK with that.

Having divorced parents can be really hard at first. But it gets easier. I used to wish Mom and Dad would get back together. But now I know they are happy being apart. I have learned that I can still be happy, too.

Meet Joseph

Hello! I'm Joseph. I live in Connecticut with my mom, sister, and three brothers. We have a cat named Solay. I like to code and play video games. Learning about wild cats and other animals is also fun. Because I love animals, I want to help them. I want to be a zoologist or wildlife biologist when I grow up.

Respecting People Who Have Divorced Parents

Your friends with divorced parents might not always be able to play with you. They might be visiting their other parent.

Be mindful of what you say and do. Support your friend. They might be going through a tough time.

Remember that every family is unique. What works for some families does not work for others.

Divorce is not a child's fault. Do not blame them for the divorce.

Your friend might feel sad, angry, and confused. That is normal. Let them talk about their feelings.

Helpful Terms

coding Programming a computer to follow a set of instructions.

divorce To end a marriage by a court.

shelter A safe place for people to stay for a short time.

sibling A brother or a sister.

Read More

Atkins, Sue. *The Divorce Journal for Kids.* London: Jessica Kingsley Publishers, 2021.

Dellaccio, Tanya. *Families with a Single Parent.* New York: PowerKids Press, 2021.

Finne, Stephanie. *Facing Divorce.* Minneapolis: Jump!, 2021.

Websites

KIDSHEALTH: COPING WITH SAD FEELINGS
https://kidshealth.org/en/kids/sadness.html
Learn how to deal with sadness people might feel during a divorce.

RESOURCES: HELP FOR KIDS OF DIVORCE
https://divorceandchildren.com/resources/help-for-kids-of-divorce
A helpful list of books and films to help kids understand divorce.

SESAME WORKSHOP: DIVORCE
https://sesameworkshop.org/topics/divorce
Visit this website for many resources about divorce.

THE SPLIT OUTREACH PROJECT
https://www.splitfilm.org
Watch these films to hear kids' stories and feelings about divorce.

Every effort has been made to ensure that these websites are appropriate for children. However, because of the nature of the Internet, it is impossible to guarantee that these sites will remain active indefinitely or that their contents will not be altered.